I DEDICATE THIS BOOK TO

MY BEAUTIFUL WIFE CAROLYN

Thank you for pushing me forward and never letting me give up. You are the O-H to my I-O.

DANNY JR.

For being an awesome son. I pray you develop a love for reading and an overactive imagination like me. There's nothing wrong with daydreams and doodles.

NANA

Thank you for supporting my dream and being just as excited as I am, if not more so.

MY THIRD GRADE CLASSES

For listening and laughing, even if it wasn't funny.

www.mascotbooks.com

The Scarlet Cleat

For more information, please contact:
Mascot Books
560 Herndon Parkway #120
Herndon, VA 20170
info@mascotbooks.com

CPSIA Code: PRT0417A
ISBN-13: 978-1-63177-955-8

Printed in the United States

THE SCARLET CLEAT

By Danny Kelley

This is the story of a little **BUCKEYE** named Fubsy Lento. Fubsy was a sweet little nut who was invisible to most people, but he had a dream deep down inside his shell. One day, he was going to play football for **THE OHIO STATE BUCKEYES**.

Fubsy's two older step-brothers, Brock and Brick, were the complete opposite of Fubsy. They were strong, quick, and robust, and Fubsy was fragile, slow, and meek. But they all had one thing in common: they wanted to play for the nationally feared **OHIO STATE BUCKEYES.**

But while Brock and Brick spent hours lifting weights, training, and practicing their football skills, Fubsy was stuck cleaning sweat-soaked jerseys, scrubbing floors, and cooking enormous meals for his ravenous step-brothers.

It had always been this way because Fubsy was so small, but deep down he knew he had the skills to compete with the big boys. He just **had to find a way**.

One day, as Fubsy was washing Brock and Brick's vomit-inducing gear, he heard an announcement over the radio.

"This Saturday at The Shoe, the **BUCKEYES** will be holding open tryouts from 9:00 in the morning until noon. Remember to bring your own gear and be ready to show off your football skills!"

"Wow! I actually have a chance to try out for the **BUCKEYES**!" said Fubsy, throwing down the disgusting laundry he was doing. "I've got to practice! Where are Brick and Brock?"

He found his step-brothers outside lifting weights. "Are you guys practicing for the tryouts this weekend?" he asked. "Because I'm going to try out too. Can I join?"

"**YOU??**" Brick laughed.

"Can you imagine him out there?!" yelled Brock. "Hooo! Sure, Fubsy you can come try out...**TO BE THE FOOTBALL!**"

"Good one, Brock!" yelled Brick. "We could punt you farther than you could throw the ball!"

Fubsy ran teary-eyed past his terrible step-brothers and back to his room. "I'll never play football," he cried. "I'll never make the **BUCKEYES!**"

Suddenly, an explosion of scarlet smoke surrounded Fubsy, and the ear-piercing **PHWEEEEET!** of a whistle split the air.

"Sweet fancy wolverines! What's happening?!" Fubsy called out, looking through the smoke. He could barely make out a figure standing, no, floating in front of him!

"Get up off the floor," commanded a gruff voice, "and show some grit, son. This ol' whistle ain't that loud!"

"Who, no, **what**, are you?" Fubsy asked.

"What am I? Sheesh, I'm your Fairy Godcoach, Woody! I heard your cries and came as soon as these dusty old wings would let me. Had to find my whistle too. Turns out it was around my neck the whole time!"

"My fairy what? Godcoach?" questioned Fubsy.

"That's right! I'm your Fairy Godcoach and I've come to help you get ready for tryouts."

Fubsy's mouth fell to the floor. "No way. You're going to help ME? **I CAN'T BELIEVE IT!**"

"I like your spunk, kid," said Woody. "We've only got one week, so let's go! **ABRACA-HIKE!**" And with that, Woody and Fubsy magically appeared in Ohio Stadium.

For the rest of the week, Woody and Fubsy did nothing but practice: catching, running, juking, breaking tackles, and most importantly, touchdown dancing. With a **"BiPpity-Hut, BippiTy-HikE!"** Fubsy had a field of fairy football players to zip around.

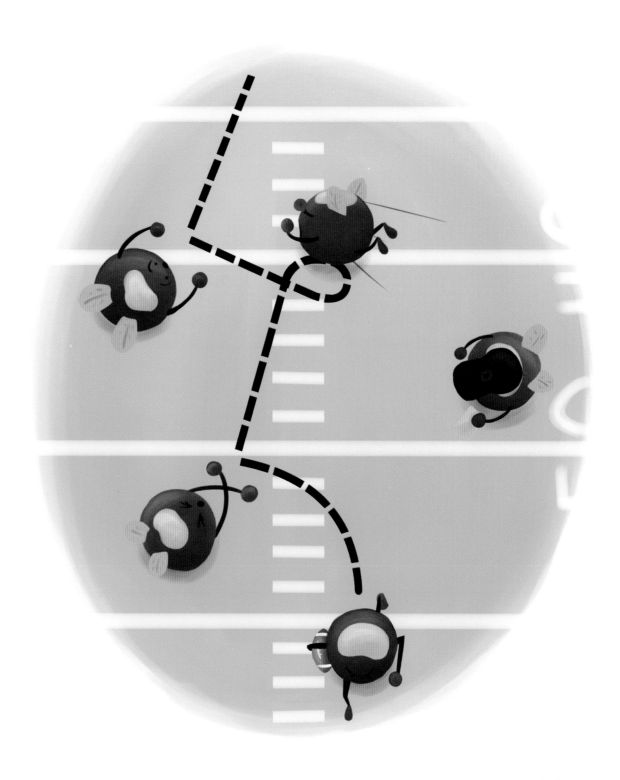

Woody kept Fubsy on his toes, making him sprint as fast as he could down the line while conjuring obstacles out of thin air. Fubsy held the football tight and juked left and right all the way to the endzone.

At the end of the week, Woody looked at Fubsy with a twinkle of pride in his eye and said in his gravelly voice, "Okay kid, **I THINK YOU'RE READY**. I'll see you at tryouts tomorrow."

Fubsy wiped the sweat from his brow and looked up just in time to see Woody disappear with a PUFF of smoke.

As soon as Fubsy got up the next morning, he could hear his step-brothers getting their gear ready to go.

Suddenly, he panicked. **"I DON'T HAVE ANY GEAR!"** he cried. He began a frantic search for anything he could find. But the only things he found were an old pair of holey shoes, pants that wouldn't stay up, a jersey so dirty you couldn't read the team name, and a helmet covered with massive dents. He put them on anyway.

Just then, Woody appeared out of nowhere. "What's all this?" he questioned.

"It's the best I could do, Woody," said Fubsy. "I can't go to tryouts like this. I can't even move in these."

"You're going to these tryouts and you're going to show everyone what you can do!" Woody barked. Then he waved his wand and cried,

"Ala-ka-hut, Ala-ka-hike!"

The whole room was covered in a scarlet and gray cloud of smoke.

When it lifted, Fubsy was clad in all new football gear!

A **gleaming** new helmet was on his head, and on his back was a scarlet jersey with a gray number 1. He was wearing **perfectly fitted** gray pants and his feet fit snugly into a brand new pair of **shiny** scarlet cleats. He was speechless.

Woody's normally stoic face gave the briefest of smiles, then he gruffly said, "You better get going and show those coaches what a real football star looks like."

"**YES**, **SIR!**" cried Fubsy, running out the door. "**THANK YOU, SIR!**"

"But Fubsy," Woody yelled after him, "be sure to leave before the campus bell tolls noon and tryouts are over!"

When Fubsy arrived at Ohio Stadium, he strode bravely onto the manicured field, passing the snickers of the other players who were twice, or even three times the size of him. But he took a deep breath, and knew he was where he belonged.

PHWEEET!

The whistle blew for the first drill and Fubsy exploded off the line. It was the 40-yard dash and Fubsy was flying like a bolt of lightning with wings. He reached the finish line first! The coach's whistle fell from his mouth as the other players crossed the line several seconds later. They were in shock at the tiny nut too, their eyes wide. Fubsy just calmly smiled to himself; he was ready for the next drill.

At each station, Fubsy shocked coaches and players. HOW COULD SOMEONE SO small BE SO GOOD?

Coach Brutus in particular was following him from station to station, stopping to take notes and confer with a huddle of assistant coaches. Soon it was time for a scrimmage.

"Team Gray will be on offense," Coach Brutus began, "and Team Scarlet will be on defense. Coach Trimble will assign defensive positions and Coach Wadsworth will assign the offensive positions."

As Coach Wadsworth explained positions, Coach Brutus pointed at Fubsy and said, "I want him in the running back position, got it?"

"IF YOU SAY SO, COACH," said Coach Wadsworth, taking another look at Fubsy. "Number 1, guess you're in."

"LET'S GO!"

"Hut, **hut**, **hike!**" shouted the quarterback, as the ball was snapped and he dropped back to throw. The offensive line was quickly overrun by the defense and the quarterback was sacked in no time.

"**TEAM GRAY!** Get your heads in the game!" shouted Coach Wadsworth. "You all better show me something better than this before I find some players with a little more spirit!"

The offense screamed, **"Yessir!"** and quickly huddled to devise a new plan.

"All right, boys," barked the quarterback, "we need to change this up. Let's try a handoff to number 1 here and we'll see what happens. You ready, small fry?"

"I was born ready!" Fubsy barked fiercely, taking his position in the backfield. He could feel his heart pounding as the quarterback called for the ball.

Fubsy BURST forward, cleanly taking the handoff from the quarterback. He tucked the ball neatly under his arm and sprinted behind his blockers. He quickly found a hole and burst through.

Suddenly, a defensive linebacker was in his path! Fubsy SPUN to the left and moved past him easily. Next up, a safety was getting ready for the tackle. Fubsy JUKED right, then left, then went right on through the defender's legs, leaving him grasping thin air before falling flat on his face. Fubsy could hear the thundering of feet behind him as he closed in on the endzone. He was so close he could **feel** it!

Fubsy was at the **15**, the **10**, the **5**... **TOUCHDOWN!**

A cheer went up from the offense as Fubsy crossed the goal line. Moments later, Fubsy's cheering teammates swept him up, congratulating him and marveling at his fancy footwork.

Suddenly, the campus bells began to toll noon.

Uh-oh, thought Fubsy, *it's time for me to get out of here!*

Coach Brutus was headed toward him with a huge smile on his face. But Fubsy couldn't wait around, his uniform was already deteriorating and he could feel his Fairy Godcoach's magic beginning to wear off. He took off out of the crowd and out of the stadium. As he left, one of his brilliant scarlet cleats came loose and fell off on the stadium steps.

Back on the field, Coach Brutus searched everywhere for Fubsy. "Where did that **BUCKEYE** go?" he asked. **"FIND HIM!"** Soon players and coaches were combing the stadium looking for the speedy little nut.

After searching everywhere, Coach Wadsworth ran up to Coach Brutus and cried, "Coach, we couldn't find that little **BUCKEYE** anywhere. But we did find this **scarlet cleat**. I think it's his!"

"Well, I'll be!" exclaimed Coach Brutus. "Where in the world did that **BUCKEYE** go? He's our key to victory this season! I'm going to go door to door with this scarlet cleat until I find the lightning quick feet that fit this shoe!"

So off Coach Brutus went, trekking across Columbus, asking everyone he saw to try on the scarlet cleat.

For a week straight Coach Brutus searched to no avail, and as he neared the last street in Columbus, he had almost given up hope. He had to find that lightning quick **BUCKEYE** with the scarlet cleats. How else would his team be able to win?

At the very last house on the block, two large **BUCKEYES** were lifting weights in the yard.

"Hello there!" called out Coach Brutus. "Would you **BUCKEYES** come try on this cleat for me? I'm looking for the football star whose foot this cleat belongs to."

Brock and Brick looked at each other, then immediately ran toward Coach Brutus, STUMBLING, **BITING**, and **CLAWING** to be the first one to try on the cleat.

"Give me that shoe! It'll fit my foot for sure!" said Brock as he tried to shove the scarlet cleat onto his oversized foot. But only three of his toes fit into the shoe!

"Let me see that cleat!" bellowed Brick, holding his nose and wiping tears from his eyes before grabbing the cleat from his brother. Brick gave the cleat a shove onto his foot, but only two of his toes would fit!

"AAAAAUUUGGHH!" yelled Brick. In his rage, he chucked the scarlet cleat into the air and it soared clean over the roof and out of sight.

"OUCH!" came a voice from the backyard.

"What on earth was that?" questioned Coach Brutus. "Did that cleat just hit someone back there?"

"Oh, I'm sure it was just Fubsy. He's back there handwashing our delicate jerseys," said Brock.

"Maybe if we're lucky it knocked him out," said Brick, making a point to flex his muscles in front of Coach Brutus. "I do have a good arm, especially for footballs."

Coach Brutus was not impressed. "You boys are a piece of work. I'll tell you now, you'd never make it on my team with attitudes like that. I'm going to check on your brother."

Coach **Brutus** rounded the corner and found Fubsy in a daze holding the scarlet cleat and rubbing his bruised head.

"Excuse me son, are you all right? I guess that clonked you on the noggin after all."

"Uhhh…" mumbled Fubsy, still disoriented. "Well, uh, yeah I guess it did. I'll be all right, but what are you doing here, sir, and how did Brick find my missing cleat?"

"YOUR CLEAT?!" asked Coach **Brutus** in excitement. "You mean that scarlet cleat belongs to **you?**"

"Well yeah," said Fubsy. "I had these on the other day at tryouts, but I had to leave early. I guess I left this behind."

"Please, please try it on! I must be sure it belongs to you," said Coach Brutus.

"Okay," said Fubsy, and he slipped the scarlet cleat onto his foot. It was as snug and perfect of a fit as a cleat could get.

"**O-H!** I don't believe my eyes!" cried Coach Brutus in awe. "I've been searching for you for days! You were the greatest player I'd ever seen! Those feet, I've never seen feet move so quickly. I need you on our team! **Will you please come play for me?**"

Fubsy could hardly believe what he was hearing!

"OF COURSE I'LL PLAY FOR THE BUCKEYES!" Fubsy shouted. "It's always been my dream to call you my coach! I can't believe this!" Fubsy couldn't contain his excitement as he half tackled, half bear-hugged Coach Brutus in joy.

And with that, Fubsy Lento joined **THE OHIO STATE BUCKEYES!** He soon led the team to not only **one**, but **two** undefeated seasons. His step-brothers finally learned what an amazing player he was and realized the error of their ways. They groveled for forgiveness and repented their evil treatment of Fubsy over the years. Fubsy, being a kind little **BUCKEYE**, forgave them and even enjoyed seeing Brock and Brick at every one of his games, wearing his number in scarlet and gray and cheering him on from the stands.

Fubsy Lento was voted **MVP** and was finally living his dream. And if you look closely you just might see Fairy Godcoach Woody beaming with pride as Fubsy runs down the field.

ABOUT THE AUTHOR

DANNY KELLEY has spent the majority of his life in the great state of Ohio. He attended The Ohio State University and received his B.S. in Education in 2011, and then received his M. Ed. in 2012. Danny currently teaches third grade and is in his fourth year of teaching.

Danny resides in Marysville, Ohio, with his beautiful wife, Carolyn, and his son, Danny Jr. It has always been Danny's dream to publish a book that his son would enjoy reading.

When he's not writing, illustrating, or teaching, Danny can be found enjoying the outdoors, cooking, playing with his two dogs, Harvey and Elmer, or wrangling one of the many chickens on the Kelley farm.